Ride a Cock Horse

And Other Nursery Rhymes

with illustrations by

Mervyn Peake

The British Library

First published in 1940 by Chatto & Windus

This edition published in 2015 by
The British Library
96 Euston Road
London NW1 2DB

Illustrations copyright © Estate of Mervyn Peake

British Library Cataloguing in Publication Data
A catalogue record for this book is available from
the British Library

ISBN 978 0 7123 5786 9

Cover by Tony Antoniou, British Library Design Office
Printed in Hong Kong by Great Wall Printing Co. Ltd

Contents

Ride a Cock-Horse   *page*   2

Rub-a-Dub-Dub   4

Old King Cole   6

I Had a Little Nut Tree   8

How Many Miles to Babylon ?   10

I Saw a Ship A-Sailing   12

The Man in the Wilderness   14

Doctor Foster Went to Glo'ster   16

Sing a Song of Sixpence   18

I Had a Little Husband   20

Little Jack Horner   22

Jack Sprat   24

Where are you going to my Pretty Maid ?   26

I Saw a Peacock   28

Ride a Cock-Horse

Ride a cock-horse to Banbury Cross,
To see a fine lady on a white horse ;
Rings on her fingers and bells on her toes,
She shall have music wherever she goes.

Rub-a-Dub-Dub

Rub-a-dub-dub,
Three men in a tub,
And who do you think they be?
The butcher; the baker;
The candle-stick maker;
Turn 'em out knaves all three.

Old King Cole

Old King Cole was a merry old soul,
And a merry old soul was he;
He called for his pipe,
And he called for his bowl,
And he called for his fiddlers three.

Every fiddler, he had a fiddle
And a very fine fiddle had he;
Oh, there's none so rare
As can compare
With King Cole and his fiddlers three.

Mervyn Peake.

I Had a Little Nut Tree

I had a little nut tree,
Nothing would it bear,
But a silver nutmeg,
And a golden pear.
The King of Spain's daughter
Came to visit me,
And all was because of
My little nut tree.

How Many Miles to Babylon?

"How many miles to Babylon?"
"Three score and ten."
"Can I get there by candle-light?"
"Ay, and back again."

I Saw a Ship A-Sailing

I saw a ship a-sailing,
A-sailing on the sea;
And Oh! it was all laden
With pretty things for thee!

There were comfits in the cabin,
And apples in the hold;
The sails were made of silk,
And the masts were made of gold.

The Man in the Wilderness

The man in the wilderness asked me
How many strawberries grew in the sea:
I answered him, as I thought good,
As many as red herrings grew in the
wood.

Doctor Foster went to Glo'ster

Doctor Foster went to Glo'ster
In a shower of rain ;
He stepped in a puddle,
Up to the middle,
And never went there again.

Sing a Song of Sixpence

Sing a song of sixpence,
A pocket full of rye;
Four and twenty blackbirds
Baked in a pie.
When the pie was opened
The birds began to sing,
Was not that a dainty dish
To set before the King?

The King was in his counting-house,
Counting out his money;
The Queen was in the parlour
Eating bread and honey;
The maid was in the garden
Hanging out the clothes,
When down there came a blackbird
And pecked off her nose.

I Had a Little Husband

I had a little husband
No bigger than my thumb;
I put him in a pint pot,
And there I bid him drum.

I gave him some garters
To gather up his hose,
And a little pocket handkerchief
To wipe his pretty nose.

I bought a little horse
That galloped up and down;
I bridled him and saddled him,
And sent him out of town.

Little Jack Horner

Little Jack Horner
 Sat in the corner,
Eating his Christmas pie.
 He put in his thumb,
And pulled out a plum,
And said "What a good boy am I."

Jack Sprat

Jack Sprat could eat no fat,
His wife could eat no lean;
And so betwixt the two of them
They licked the platter clean.

Jack ate all the lean,
Joan ate all the fat,
The bone they picked it clean,
And gave it to the cat.

Where are you going to my Pretty Maid?

"Where are you going to my pretty maid?"
"I'm going a-milking, sir," she said.

"May I go with you, my pretty maid?"
"You're kindly welcome, sir," she said.

"What is your father, my pretty maid?"
"My father's a farmer, sir," she said.

"What is your fortune, my pretty maid?"
"My face is my fortune, sir," she said.

"Then I can't marry you, my pretty maid!"
"Nobody asked you, sir!" she said.

I Saw a Peacock

I saw a peacock with a fiery tail
I saw a blazing comet drop down hail
I saw a cloud wrapped with ivy round
I saw an oak creep on along the ground
I saw a pismire swallow up a whale
I saw the sea brim full of ale
I saw a Venice glass five fathom deep
I saw a well full of men's tears that weep
I saw red eyes all of a flaming fire
I saw a house bigger than the moon
                              and higher
I saw the sun at twelve o'clock at night
I saw the man that saw this wondrous
                              sight.